A Story That's Part Spanish, Part English, and a Whole Lot of Fun

We Laugh ALIKE JUNTOS nos reímos

Carmen T. Bernier-Grand

Illustrated by / Ilustrado por **Alyssa Bermudez**

ini Charlesbridge

Para mis nietos: Ricardo, Rey, Paloma, Perlita, Roselito y AnaLis—C. T. B-G.

For my nephew, Alex—A. B.

Text copyright © 2021 by Carmen T. Bernier-Grand
Illustrations copyright © 2021 by Alyssa Bermudez

At the time of publication, all URLs printed in this book were accurate and active.
Charlesbridge, the author, and the illustrator are not responsible for the content or accessibility of any website.

Published by Charlesbridge
9 Galen Street
Watertown, MA 02472
(617) 926-0329
www.charlesbridge.com

Library of Congress Cataloging-in-Publication Data
Names: Bernier-Grand, Carmen T., author. | Bermudez, Alyssa, illustrator
Title: We laugh alike / Juntos nos reímos: A story that's part Spanish, part English, and a whole lot of fun / Carmen T. Bernier-Grand;
illustrated by Alyssa Bermudez.
Other titles: Juntos nos reímos
Description: Watertown, MA : Charlesbridge, [2021] | Text in English and Spanish. | Summary: Six children are at the park,
one group speaks only English and the other only Spanish, but soon they learn to communicate through playing, dancing, and singing.
Identifiers: LCCN 2018058515 (print) | LCCN 2019012991 (ebook) | ISBN 9781632898470 (ebook) | ISBN 9781623540968 (reinforced for library use)
Subjects: LCSH: Language and languages—Juvenile fiction. | Friendship—Juvenile fiction. | Communication—Juvenile fiction. |
Play—Juvenile fiction. | CYAC: Language and languages—Fiction. | Friendship—Fiction. | Communication—Fiction. | Play—Fiction. |
Spanish language materials—Bilingual.
Classification: LCC PZ73 (ebook) | LCC PZ73 .B412 2021 (print) | DDC
[E]—dc23 LC record available at https://lccn.loc.gov/2018058515

Printed in China
(hc) 10 9 8 7 6 5 4 3 2 1

Illustrations created digitally using scanned textures and Adobe Photoshop
Display type set in Roger by Tail Spin Studio
Text type set in Colby Condensed by Jason Vandenberg
Color separations by Colourscan Print Co Pte Ltd, Singapore
Printed by 1010 Printing International Limited in Huizhou, Guangdong, China
Production supervision by Brian G. Walker
Designed by Jacqueline Noelle Cote and Kristen Nobles

TODAY we are not alone in the park. Three other kids just showed up.

HOY no estamos solos en el parque.
Hay otros tres niños jugando.

We listen to the other kids, even though we don't understand a word of Spanish.

Escuchamos a los tres niños,
aunque no sabemos inglés.

We haven't heard their songs before.
We like their rhythms.

Nunca habíamos oído sus canciones.
Nos gustan esos ritmos.

We don't know how to dance like they do.
We watch to learn the steps.

No sabemos bailar como ellos.
Los observamos para aprender los pasos.

Quizás quieran saltar con nosotros.

Salto la cuerda:
uno, dos y tres.
Cuento los saltos:
cuatro, cinco y seis.

Salta conmigo,
cuenta con los pies.
Salta tú ahora:
siete, ocho, nueve y diez.

They know how to jump rope!
But we don't understand their rhyme.

Nuestra rima los invita a saltar
con nosotros, pero no nos hacen caso.

OK, we'll jump rope, too.

Clap your hands!
Stamp your feet!
Come on, everybody.
Jump with me.
One, two, three,
four, five, six!

Our rhyme invites them
to jump with us.
But they don't join in.

But then . . .
Pero entonces . . .

They gesture for us to play!
Nos invitan a jugar.

Nos siguen cuando corremos,
y se suben con nosotros al carrusel.
  We chase them to the merry-go-round.
Giramos y giramos.
  Round and round we go!

Cuando el carrusel se detiene y
nos bajamos, caemos al suelo, mareados.
When the merry-go-round stops, we get off.
We are dizzy, and we fall.
Nos reímos a carcajadas.
We burst out laughing.

Sentados en el suelo, tejemos coronas de diente de león.

Sitting on the ground, we make dandelion crowns.

Nos coronamos unos a otros.

We crown each other.

Corremos a nuestros tronos: ¡los columpios!
We run to our thrones: the swings!
¡Más alto! Hasta que nuestros pies toquen el cielo.
High! Higher! All the way to the sky!

¡Vengan todos!
Vamos a saltar.
Saltemos la cuerda
doce veces más.

Clap your hands.
Stamp your feet.
Come on, everybody.
Jump with me.
Until twelve
it must be!

Uno, dos, tres, cuatro.
One, two, three, four.

Cinco, seis, siete, ocho.
Five, six, seven, eight.
Nueve, diez, once, ¡doce!
Nine, ten, eleven, twelve!

¡Ja! ¡Ja! ¡Ja!
¡Contamos en inglés!
　　Ha! Ha! Ha!
　　We counted in Spanish!
¡Ja! ¡Ja! ¡Ja!
Juntos nos reímos.
　　Ha! Ha! Ha!
　　We laugh alike.

Cantamos la misma canción un millón de veces
hasta que aprenden las palabras
y cantan con nosotros.

We sing the same song a million times
until they learn the words
and sing with us.

"¡Hasta mañana, amigos!"
les gritamos cuando se van.

"See you tomorrow!"
we yell when we leave.

GLOSARIO / GLOSSARY

aplaude / clap your hands
bailar / dance
salta / jump
carcajada / burst of laughter
carrusel / merry-go-round
canciones / songs
cielo / sky
columpio / swing
con nosotros / with us
contamos / we counted
coronas / crowns
corremos / we run
cuerda / rope

diente de león / dandelion
entonces / then
español / Spanish
giramos / we go around
gritamos / we yell
igual / alike
inglés / English
invitar / to invite
jugando / playing
juntos / together
mareados / dizzy
misma(o) / same
no entendemos / we don't understand

no sabemos / we don't know
palabras / words
parque / park
pasos / steps
perseguir / to chase
reímos / we laugh
rima / rhyme
ritmos / rhythms
salta conmigo / jump with me
tronos / thrones
vengan todos / come on,
everybody
zapatea / stamp your feet

UNA NOTA PARA TI

Los idiomas son para comunicarse. Si estás aprendiendo un nuevo idioma y alguien se ríe porque dijiste incorrectamente una palabra o la pronunciaste con un acento, no te preocupes. ¡No te rindas! Continúa aprendiendo ese idioma. Aprende a hablarlo, a leerlo, a escribirlo. Te aseguro que vas a hacer nuevos amigos.

Hay más de 6,900 idiomas en el mundo. Probablemente no vas a poder aprenderlos todos. Pero hay otros métodos de comunicación. Cuando invitas a otros a jugar, a bailar y a cantar, puedes hacer amigos. Los vas a entender, aunque no sepan tu idioma, porque todos reímos juntos.

A NOTE FOR YOU

Language exists so that we can communicate with one another. If you are learning a new language and somebody laughs because you say a word incorrectly or pronounce it with an accent, that's their problem, not yours. Don't give up! Learn to speak that language; learn to read it; learn to write it. If you do, I assure you that you will make new friends.

There are more than 6,900 languages in the world, so you probably won't learn them all. But there are other ways to communicate, too. When you invite others to play, dance, and sing, you can make friends. You will understand them, even if they don't know your language, because we all laugh alike.